To all the poorly children in the world
K. G.

To my family
M. McQ.

Published in 2000 by The Millbrook Press, Inc.,
2 Old New Milford Road, Brookfield, Connecticut 06804

First published in the United Kingdom 2000 as *Who's Poorly, Too?*
by The Bodley Head Children's Books
Random House, 20 Vauxhall Bridge Road, London SW1V 2SA

Library of Congress Cataloging-in-publication Data

Gray, Kes.
The get well soon book : good wishes for bad times / Kes Gray & Mary McQuillan.
p. cm.
Summary: Cynthia the centipede, Harold the hamster, Tiffany the turtle, and other
animals suffer from various injuries or illnesses.
ISBN 0-7613-1922-0 (lib. bdg.) - ISBN 0-7613-1435-0 (trade)
[1. Wounds and injuries- Fiction. 2. Sick--Fiction. 3. Animals--Fiction.] I. McQuillan,
Mary. II. Title.

PZ7.G77928 2000
[E]--dc21
                                                                    00-027147

Printed in Singapore
1 3 5 4 2

The Get Well Soon Book

Good Wishes for Bad Times

KES GRAY & MARY MCQUILLAN

The Millbrook Press
Brookfield, Connecticut

Poor Cynthia the centipede.

KENNEDY

She sprained 98 ankles playing field hockey.

Poor Harry the hamster.

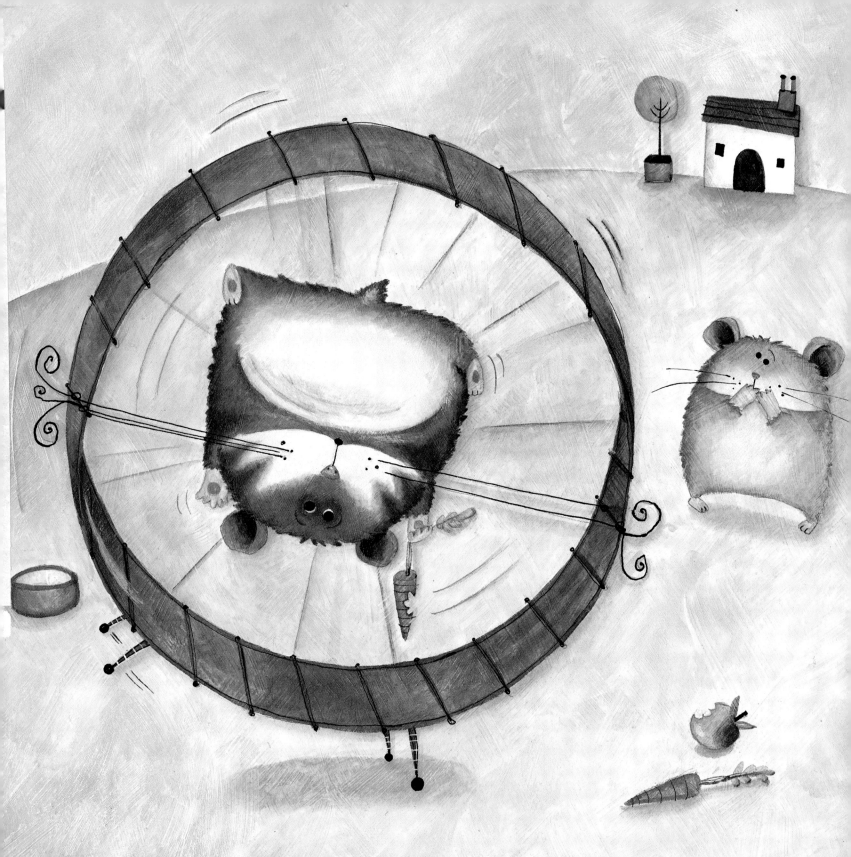

His whiskers got caught in his wheel.

Poor Tiffany the turtle.

An elephant stepped right on her shell.

Poor Marco the mole.

He tunneled into a brick wall.

Poor Danny the dalmatian.

He broke out into stripes.

Poor Paul the python.

A gorilla tied him up in a knot.

Poor Katie the cat.

She tried to chase a mouse through
a mouse hole.

Poor Pedro the penguin.

He forgot to break the ice before diving in.

Poor Connie the crocodile.

She broke her tooth biting a rhino.

KENNEDY

Poor Delia the dragon.

She sneezed and burned herself.

But they all followed the doctor's orders,

and they all took their medicine,

and they all got better in . . .

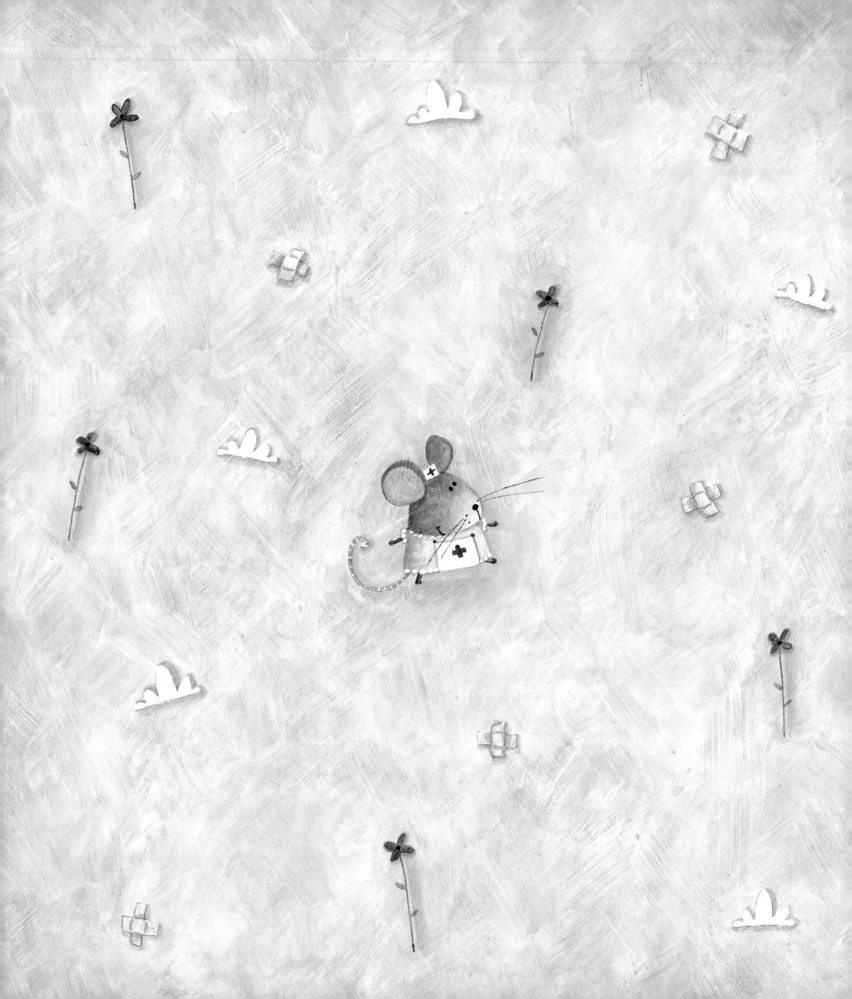